Hattie and the Fox

story by Mem Fox

pictures by Patricia Mullins

D.C. Heath and Company
Lexington, Massachusetts / Toronto, Ontario

Acknowledgments

Grateful acknowledgment is made for permission to reprint the following copyrighted material.

HATTIE AND THE FOX, by Mem Fox and illustrated by Patricia Mullins. Text copyright © 1986 by Mem Fox. Illustrations copyright © 1986 by Patricia Mullins. First American Edition, 1987.

This edition is reprinted by arrangement with Macmillan Publishing Company, a division of Macmillan, Inc.

Printed simultaneously in Canada

Printed in the United States of America

International Standard Book Number: 0-669-30230-9

2 3 4 5 6 7 8 9 10 - POO - 96 95 94 93

Hattie was a big black hen.

One morning she looked up and said,

"Goodness gracious me!

I can see a nose

in the bushes!"

3

"Good grief!" said the goose.

"Well, well!" said the pig.

"Who cares?" said the sheep.

"So what?" said the horse.

"What next?" said the cow.

And Hattie said,
"Goodness gracious me!
I can see a nose and
two eyes in the bushes!"

"Good grief!" said the goose.

"Well, well!" said the pig.

"Who cares?" said the sheep.

"So what?" said the horse.

"What next?" said the cow.

And Hattie said,
"Goodness gracious me!

I can see a nose, two eyes,
and two ears in the bushes!"

"Good grief!" said the goose.

"Well, well!" said the pig.

"Who cares?" said the sheep.

"So what?" said the horse.

"What next?" said the cow.

And Hattie said,

"Goodness gracious me!

I can see a nose, two eyes, two ears, and two legs in the bushes!"

"Good grief!" said the goose.

"Well, well!" said the pig.

"Who cares?" said the sheep.

"So what?" said the horse.

"What next?" said the cow.

19

And Hattie said,

"Goodness gracious me!

I can see a nose, two eyes, two ears, two legs,

and a body in the bushes!"

"Good grief!" said the goose.

"Well, well!" said the pig.

"Who cares?" said the sheep.

"So what?" said the horse.

"What next?" said the cow.

And Hattie said,

"Goodness gracious me!

I can see a nose, two eyes, two ears, a body,

four legs, and a tail in the bushes!

It's a fox! It's a fox!"

And she flew very quickly into a nearby tree.

"Oh, no!" said the goose.

"Dear me!" said the pig.

"Oh dear!" said the sheep.

"Oh, help!" said the horse.

But the cow said, "MOO!"

so loudly that the fox was
frightened and ran away.

And they were all so surprised
that none of them said anything
for a very long time.